A gift for

_____

from

_____

Eve Bunting   Illustrated by **Judy Love**

The Baby Shower

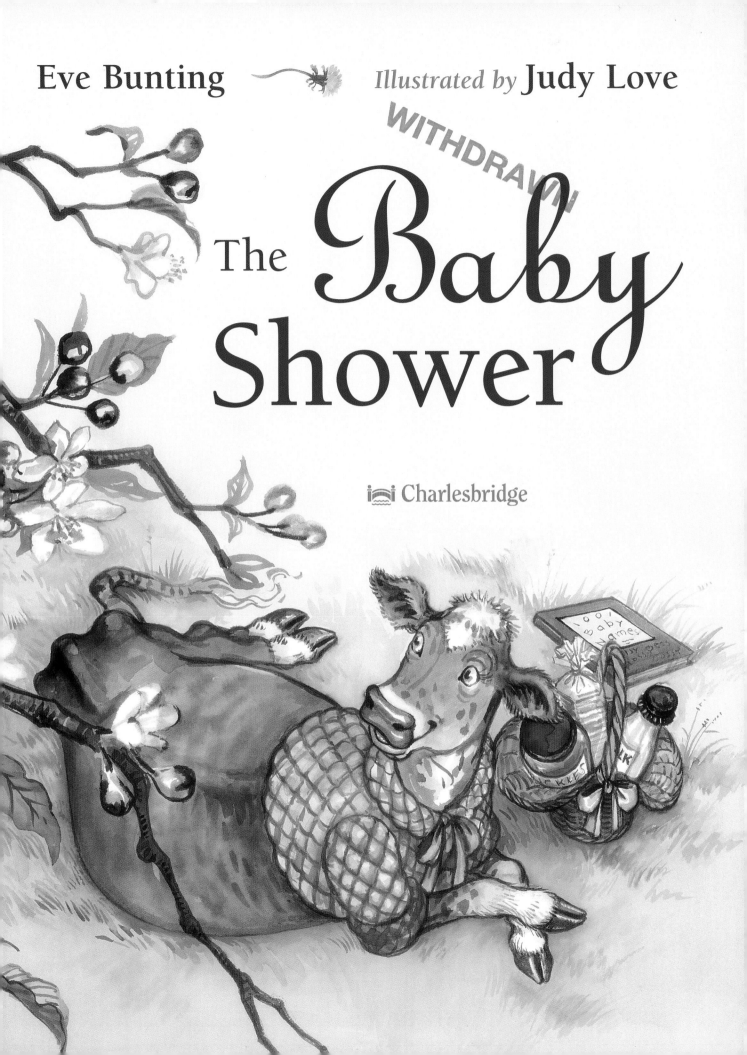

ɪɴɪ Charlesbridge

To my cousin, Joan Geating, with love
—E. B.

In loving memory of my parents, Dorothy Winchell and Donald E. Love
—J. L.

Published by Charlesbridge
85 Main Street
Watertown, MA 02472
(617) 926-0329
www.charlesbridge.com

Library of Congress Cataloging-in-Publication Data
Bunting, Eve, 1928–
The Baby shower / Eve Bunting ; illustrated by Judy Love.
p. cm.
Summary: When news spreads that Ms. Brindle Cow is having her baby,
many animals travel to share her joy, only to be greeted with a big surprise.
ISBN 978-1-58089-139-4 (reinforced for library use)
[1. Cows—Fiction. 2. Animals—Infancy—Fiction. 3. Animals—Fiction.
4. Birthdays—Fiction. 5. Stories in rhyme.] I. Love, Judith DuFour, ill. II. Title.
PZ8.3.B92Bab 2007
[E]—dc22   2006020950

Printed in China
(hc) 10 9 8 7 6 5 4 3 2 1

Illustrations done in transparent inks on Arches watercolor paper
Display type and text type set in Cathedral and Berkeley
Color separations by Chroma Graphics, Singapore
Printed and bound by Regent Publishing Services
Production supervision by Brian G. Walker
Designed by Diane M. Earley

Ms. Brindle Cow, all sweetly round,
rested on the grassy ground.
Now and then she stretched and smiled.
Soon she'd have her firstborn child.

Chipmunk got the happy word
from his friend, the small brown bird.
He told his pals, "She's far away,
so we should go this very day."

Rabbit said, "I quite remember
I had babies last September.
The first one born was such a blessing,
but more and more can be distressing!"

They started off without delay
and walked along with lots to say.
Then Turtle waved. "Hey, guys! Slow down!
I stopped to shop awhile in town."

Pig waited for them by a tree.
She said, "I'm pleased as pleased can be.
I brought this book. My piglets said
it was the best they'd ever read."

Duck waddled up. "I'm kind of slow,
but there's no doubt I want to go.
You know, of course, that I'll be there
to say the newborn-baby prayer."

Duck brought some fancy baby clothes.
Chipmunk said, "I brought a rose.
Take a sniff! It smells so sweet.
It's for the baby when we meet."

Rabbit asked, "What do you think?
I knitted booties, blue and pink."
And Turtle said, "I bought this bonnet
with pretty little pom-poms on it."

We love you, Brindle. Yes, we do.

We'll love your darling baby, too.

They walked all night. Pig had a flute
that played the sweetest tootle-toot.
They made a joyful song to bring,
an easy song they all could sing.

Mr. Bull, congratulations!
We've come to join the celebrations.

The moon and stars lit up the sky.
Fireflies came dancing by.
They kept repeating to each other,
"Brindle's going to be a mother!"

The sky grew pink and streaked with dawn.
The moon and fireflies were gone.
And there was Brindle on the grass.
Bull stood aside to let them pass.

Chipmunk gasped, "My goodness, me!
Am I seeing what I see?
This is such a sweet surprise!"
He rubbed his little chipmunk eyes.

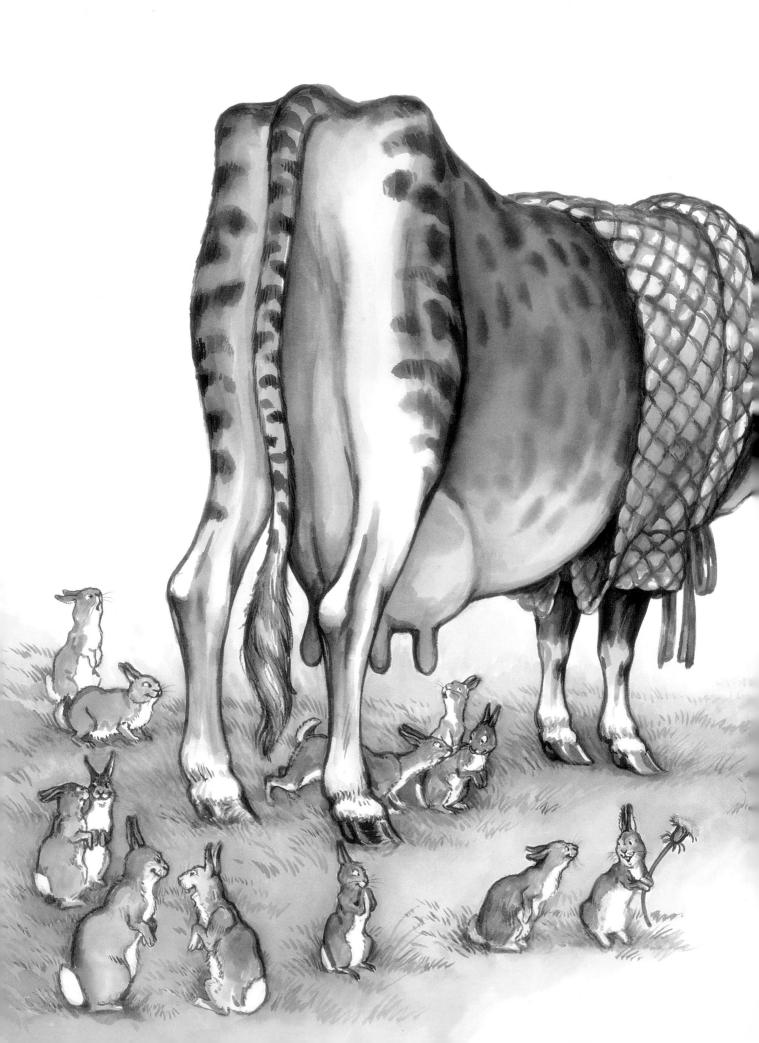

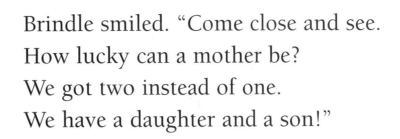

Brindle smiled. "Come close and see.
How lucky can a mother be?
We got two instead of one.
We have a daughter and a son!"

She bent and licked a small gray head,
looked at everyone, and said,
"This is May, and this is Mike.
You can kiss them if you like."

They kissed the babies and their mother.
The little bunnies kissed each other.
They gave their gifts, said "aah" and "ooh."
They gave a kiss to Daddy, too.

Duck's blessing wasn't very long,
and then they sang their joyful song.
There were words to add and words to change,
but that was easy to arrange.

We love you, Brindle. Yes, we do.
We love your darling babies, too.
Mr. Bull, congratulations!
We so enjoyed the celebrations.

We want to come again, so maybe
you could have another baby.
Baby showers are so much fun,
we'd like to have another one!

All together, shout "Hooray!"

Happy birthday, Mike and May!